Praise for

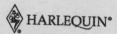 HARLEQUIN®

INTRIGUE®

from readers just like you!

"The books are filled with mystery and suspense
with the right amount of romance.
I devoured both books."
—Harlequin Intrigue reader

"It captured my attention and the romance
was just right. The suspense had me hanging
to the point where I just had to keep reading."
—Harlequin Intrigue reader

"Intrigue is my favorite genre, full of suspense
and a quick read."
—Harlequin Intrigue reader

Enjoy a sneak preview of Harlequin Intrigue for yourself.

Look for valuable coupon offers inside!

www.eHarlequin.com

Copyright © 2008 by Harlequin Books S.A.

ISBN-13: 978-0-373-15071-7
ISBN-10:   0-373-15071-7

The content of the excerpts in this book may have been edited
from their original format. The publisher acknowledges the
copyright holders of the excerpts from the individual works
as follows:

NEWBORN CONSPIRACY
Copyright © 2008 by Delores Fossen

MYSTERIOUS MILLIONAIRE
Copyright © 2008 by Kay Bergstrom

WYOMING MANHUNT
Copyright © 2008 by Ann Voss Peterson

TEXAS-SIZED SECRETS
Copyright © 2008 by Mary Jernigan

CONTENTS

HARLEQUIN

INTRIGUE

DELORES FOSSEN

FIVE-ALARM BaBies

NEWBORN CONSPIRACY

Prologue

Fall Creek, Texas

The muffled scream woke Logan McGrath.

He snapped to a sitting position in the leather recliner, turned his ear toward the sound and listened. Even through the haze of his heavy pain meds and bone-weary fatigue, he didn't have to listen long or hard to hear the raspy moans and gasps.

Someone was in a lot of pain, perhaps dying.

And that someone was on the front porch.

Because he was a man who usually dealt with worst-case scenarios, Logan automatically considered that this might be a burglar or a killer. But since he was at his brother's house in the tiny picturesque town of Fall Creek, which wasn't exactly a hotbed of criminal activity, he had to consider another possibility: that his brother, a doctor, had a visitor, a patient who was about to die on the porch. It made sense since there wasn't a hospital in town.

Just to be safe, Logan grabbed his Sig-Sauer from the end table next to him and maneuvered himself out of the chair. Not easily. It took effort. Lots of it.

He cursed the intrusion, the throbbing pain and the un-identified SOB who'd put a .38 jacketed slug in his right leg four days ago—on Christmas day, no less.

Some Christmas present.

Logan wore only his bathrobe and boxers, and he considered a detour to the guest bedroom for a shirt and shoes. But after two steps, he changed his mind. If someone was truly dying on the porch, they'd be long dead before he could get dressed and back to him.

Another moan. Another muffled scream.

Yep, he had to hurry. Logan jammed his cane onto the hardwood floor to get better traction, and with thirteen excruciating steps, he made it to the door. He aimed his gun, and braced himself for whatever he was about to have to deal with as he glanced out a side window.

The sun was just starting to set, but there was still plenty of light for him to see the blue car parked in front of his brother's isolated country house. Logan had to look down, however, to see the driver.

She was lying on the porch. Her tan wool coat and long, loose dark-green dress were hiked up to her thighs, and she had her hands clutched on her swollen, pregnant belly.

She was writhing in pain.

Logan dropped his gun onto the pine entry table, threw open the door and maneuvered himself onto the porch. It wasn't freezing but it was close and he felt the chill slide over his bare chest and feet.

She turned her head, snared his gaze, and he saw the horrible agony in her earthy brown eyes.

"Help me," she begged. Her warm breath mixed with the frigid December air and created a misty haze around her milky pale face. "My water broke when I got out of the car and the pains are already nonstop."

So, not dying. In labor. Not the end of the world but still a huge concern.

She needed a doctor *now.*

Logan turned to go back inside to make the call to 911, but she latched on to his arm and didn't let go. For such a weak-looking little thing, she had a powerful grip. She dug in her fingernails and dragged Logan down beside her.

He banged his leg on the doorjamb and could have sworn he saw stars. Still, he pushed the godawful pain aside—after some grimacing and grunting of his own—and he tried to figure out what the heck he should do.

"Who are you?" he asked.

She clamped her teeth over her bottom lip, but he still heard the groan. "It's not the time for introductions," she grumbled. She fought to rip off her panties and then threw them aside. "Help me!"

"I've never delivered a baby before," he grumbled back, but Logan knew he was in the wrong position if he stood any chance of helping her.

Another of her muffled screams got him moving. Plus, she drew blood with her fingernails. Somehow, he managed to get to the other end of her.

What Logan saw when he looked between her legs had him wanting to run for the phone again. Oh, mercy. The baby's head was already partially out and that meant they didn't have time to call an ambulance.

"I think you're supposed to push," Logan suggested. Heaven knows why he said that. Maybe he'd heard it on TV. Or maybe this was just some crazy dream brought on by prescription pain meds. Man, he hoped that's all it was.

The woman obviously didn't doubt his advice, because she pushed. *Hard.*

Logan positioned his hands under the baby's head, and he watched. That long push strained the veins on the woman's neck, and it also eased the baby out farther. He didn't just see a head but a tiny face.

Realizing he had to do something, Logan pulled off his terry-cloth robe and laid it between her legs so that the baby wouldn't land on the cold wood. It was barely in time. As the woman pushed again, the baby's shoulders and back appeared.

"One more push should do it," Logan told her.

She made a throaty, raspy sound and bore down, shoving her feet against the porch. Seconds later, the tiny baby slid right into Logan's hands.

Wow, was his first reaction.

Followed quickly by *holy hell.*

Logan had experienced a lot of crazy and amazing things in his life, but he knew this was going to go to the top of his list.

"It's a boy," he let her know.

And that baby boy had some strength because he began to cry at the top of his newborn lungs. Obviously, he wasn't having any trouble breathing on his own and Logan was thankful for that. He wouldn't have had a clue what to do if there'd been complications.

Going purely on instinct, Logan bundled the bathrobe around the baby, especially around his head, and pulled him to his chest to keep him warm.

"A boy," she repeated. She sounded both relieved and exhausted.

The woman pushed again to expel the afterbirth and

then tried to sit up. She didn't make it on her first attempt, but she did it on her second. She reached for the baby. Logan eased him into her arms.

It was strange. He immediately felt a…loss. Probably because he was freezing and the tiny baby had been warm.

The mother looked down at her newborn and smiled. It was a moment he'd remember, all right. Her, sitting there with her fiery red hair haloing her face and shoulders, and the tiny baby snuggled and crying in Logan's own bathrobe.

"My son," she whispered.

And then she said something that nearly knocked the breath out of Logan.

"He's your nephew."

Oh, man. Oh. Man. It was obviously time for him to talk to his brother.

"I'll go inside and call an ambulance," he told her. He began the maneuvering it'd take to get him up. "By the way, we should probably do those introductions now. But you obviously already know that I'm Logan McGrath."

Because he was eye level with her when he introduced himself, he saw her reaction. It was some big reaction, too. She sucked in her breath, and her mouth began to tremble.

"You can't be," she said, her voice trembling, too.

And that confused him. "My brother isn't here," he told her. "He's on rounds at the hospital in a nearby town." In addition to confusing him, she'd also captured his attention with that comment and her reaction. "Who are you? Are you a *friend* of my brother?"

She frantically shook her head and put her index finger in the baby's mouth. He began to suck and stopped crying. "I need a doctor."

He wanted answers, but they would have to wait. "Come inside," he insisted. "It's too cold out here."

"I don't think I can get up. Please, just call an ambulance."

Well, he certainly couldn't help her get to her feet. He could barely get up himself. So, Logan tried to hurry as much as he could. With lots of pain and effort, he made it back into the living room. He dialed 911, reported the incident and requested an ambulance. He also requested that they contact his brother and have him accompany that ambulance to his house.

"Get the baby and mother inside ASAP," the emergency operator insisted. "It's dangerous for a newborn to be in the cold."

Logan agreed with her, hung up, then wondered how he was going to accomplish that with his bum leg. He was more likely to fall than to be able to lift them. Still, he'd have to do it somehow.

With his cane clacking on the floor and his mind racing with possible solutions to his lack of mobility, Logan went back to the porch.

He got there just in time to see that it was empty. No mother. No newborn baby.

Just a lot of blood.

And the blue car was speeding away.

Chapter One

San Antonio, Texas
Six weeks later

Mia Crandall peered out the double glass doors of the Wilson Pediatric clinic to make sure there wasn't anyone suspicious lurking in the parking lot. There were a handful of cars, no one on the adjacent sidewalk and no one who seemed to be waiting for her to come out.

Everything was okay.

Well, everything but the niggling feeling in the pit of her stomach, but Mia had been living with that particular feeling for months now. She was beginning to wonder if it would ever go away.

She looked down at her newborn son, Tanner, and smiled. He was still sleeping, tucked in the warm, soft covers of the baby carrier. For his six-week-old checkup, Mia had dressed him in a new blue one-piece baby outfit and a matching knit cap. Still, it was winter, so she draped another blanket over the top of the carrier so he wouldn't get cold. She retrieved her pepper-spray keychain from her diaper bag and hurried out into the bitter weather.

It was already past five-thirty and the temperature had plunged since she'd first gone inside nearly an hour earlier. She'd had one of the last appointments of the day. Not accidental, but by design. The winter sun was already low in the sky and Mia hoped the duskiness would prevent her from being easily seen.

The wind slammed into her face, cutting her breath, but she kept up the fast pace until she made it to her car. During the past year, she'd learned to hurry, to stay out of plain sight, to go out as little as possible. It was second nature now.

She strapped Tanner's carrier into the rear-facing brackets mounted in the backseat and then slipped in behind the steering wheel. She started to turn on the engine, but the sound stopped her.

There was a sharp rap on the passenger's side window.

Mia's gaze whipped toward the sound and she saw a man staring at her. But this wasn't just any ordinary man.

Oh, God. He'd found her.

Choking back a gasp, Mia grabbed for the lock, but it was already too late. Logan McGrath pulled open the passenger's door and calmly got inside her car as if he had every right to do just that.

He was dressed all in black. Black pants, black pullover shirt and black leather coat. His hair was midnight black, as well, and slightly shorter than it'd been when she had seen him six weeks earlier. Maybe it was all that black attire that made his eyes stand out. They were glacier blue. Cold, hard. Demanding.

She remembered that he'd been hurt the night she had given birth to Tanner. He'd used a cane and could barely walk. But he didn't seem at a disadvantage now. She couldn't say the same for herself. He outsized her and no doubt had years of martial arts training. Still, she had something he didn't.

A maternal instinct to protect her son.

Mia forced herself not to panic. She thrust her hand in the diaper bag and located her cell phone. She was about to call 911 when Logan McGrath caught her wrist and took the phone from her. He also took her keys with the pepper spray and the diaper bag, shoving all the items on the floor next to him.

When he moved, his leather coat shifted, just a little. Enough for her to get a glimpse of the shoulder holster and gun tucked beneath it. But then, he probably didn't go many places without that firearm.

Mia lifted her chin and put some steel in her expression. There was no way she was going to let this man take control of the situation.

"Get out!" she ordered.

"Soon. I came to pick up my bathrobe. You took it with you when you left Fall Creek."

So, he obviously knew who she was. Not that he would likely forget delivering a baby on his brother's front porch. He was also obviously good with the sarcasm. Calm and cool under pressure.

Unlike her.

Her heart was beating so fast she thought it might leap out of her chest. Mia couldn't let him see that fear, though. For her baby's sake, she had to get this man out of her car. *Somehow.* And then she had to get far away from him so he could never find her again.

"I'll mail you the robe," she informed him. "Write down your address and then get out of my car."

The corner of his mouth lifted slightly. It didn't soften the rock-hard expression on his square jaw or high cheekbones. But that expression did soften when he glanced back at the infant seat.

Mia's heart dropped to her knees. God, this couldn't be happening. She'd been so stupid to go his brother's house that day. Now, that stupidity might cost her everything.

She couldn't physically fight him off, though she would try if it came down to it. However, maybe she could defuse this awful situation with some lies.

"I'm grateful to you for delivering my baby," she said, hoping that it sounded sincere. Because she was sincere about that. The rest, however, was pure fabrication. "I went to your brother's house because I was driving through Fall Creek and realized I was in labor. I saw the MD sign on his mailbox and stopped."

He turned in the seat, slowly, so that he was facing her and aimed those ice-blue eyes at her. "How do you think I found you, Mia Crandall?"

She froze. Gave it some thought. And her mouth went bone dry. Because she couldn't speak, she shook her head.

Logan McGrath calmly reached over, locked the doors, retrieved her keys and started the engine. He turned on the heater and waited until the warm air blew over them before he continued.

"I had DNA tests run on the blood you left on the porch," he explained.

Of course he had.

Logan McGrath was a man who thought like a criminal. Too bad she hadn't wiped up after herself, but then she hadn't exactly had the time or energy for that chore. Mia had barely been able to get Tanner and herself to the car so she could get to the hospital in San Antonio. During that entire drive she'd been terrified that McGrath would follow her. His injury had probably prevented that from that happening, it was highly likely that he hadn't been able to drive.

"I'm sure you know that your DNA is on file because of your former job as a counselor in a state women's shelter," he continued. "Once I had your name, I found an address for you here in San Antonio. You'd moved, of course. So, I took a different approach to locate you."

And Mia thought she might know what that *approach* was. "You hacked or bribed your way into the appointments of pediatric clinics all over the city because you knew that I'd be taking my baby in for a six weeks' checkup."

He nodded. "*Hacked* is not quite the right word. I had police assistance to help me put all the pieces together." He lifted his hands, palms up in an exaggerated gesture. "And here we are."

"Not for long." Because she needed something to do, Mia clutched the steering wheel until her knuckles turned white. "Look, if you want money because you delivered my baby—"

"You know what I want, and it's not money. It's not my robe, either. I want answers."

Mia glared at him. "No. No answers. Get out of my car and out of my life."

"That's not going to happen."

He leaned closer, violating her personal space. He smelled dangerous. And very virile, which she was sorry she'd noticed.

"Let me help you with those answers," Logan continued, his Texas drawl easy but somehow dark. "I already know a lot about you, Mia Frances Crandall. Born and raised in Dallas, you've had a tough life. When you were fifteen, two drug-crazed teen burglars broke into your home, murdered your parents and left you for dead."

Mia automatically touched her fingers to her throat, to the scar that was still there. It was faint and barely visible now. Unlike the invisible wounds beneath.

Those scars would never fade.

"I don't have time for a trip down memory lane," she grumbled. She forced back the brutal images of that night in Dallas. "I need to get home. My baby will be waking up soon and will want to nurse." Now, she leaned closer, hopefully violating his space. "Nurse, as in breast-feed. You might make your living doing shocking, violent things, but I'm guessing you'd be very uncomfortable watching me nurse Tanner."

Something went through his eyes. *"Violent things?"* He looked genuinely insulted.

Mia wanted to curse. Now, he obviously knew that she was aware of who he was. She just kept getting deeper and deeper into this hole she was digging.

"I own a private security company," he corrected.

Since there was no going back, Mia just charged forward. "You lend your services and your guns in war zones," she challenged.

"Occasionally." He lifted his shoulder. "When it's necessary to rescue people and protect American interests abroad."

Mia huffed. "That's semantics. You're an international hired gun."

"I'm the good guy." He hitched his thumb to his chest.

"That's debatable."

"Says who?" he fired right back at her.

Now, she put her thumb to her chest. "Me."

"We obviously have strong opinions about each other," he concluded. "Care to hear my opinion about you?"

"No." And Mia didn't even have to think about that.

"Tough. You're going to hear it. A little less than a year ago, right around your twenty-eighth birthday, you decided that you wanted to have a baby. There was no man in your life, no immediate prospects of marriage, so you went to Brighton Birthing Center just outside San Antonio. They have a fertility clinic there, and you made arrangements to be artificially inseminated. It was successful. You got pregnant on your first try."

He knew.

"How did you learn that?" she asked, swallowing hard.

"Careful investigative work over the past six weeks."

"It's not illegal to use artificial insemination to become pregnant. It's a private matter. And it's none of your business."

Even though she knew it was his business.

Hopefully, he didn't know that.

He opened his mouth, closed it, and waited a moment. During that moment, he looked even more annoyed. "I don't know why you did what you did, but obviously something started to go wrong. You got suspicious of the Brighton Birthing Center. So, days before the center was closed because of illegal activity, you made an appointment with your fertility counselor, and when the counselor left the room to get you a glass of water that you requested, you took some files from the counselor's desk drawer."

Mia hadn't thought it possible, but her heart beat even faster. "If I did or didn't do that, it's still none of your concern."

"But it's true. I managed to get my hands on some surveillance tapes. You took two files."

That was correct. Unfortunately, it'd also been a mistake. Mia had intended to take only her own file that day. She'd taken the other one accidentally because it had been tucked inside hers.

She wished to God that she'd never seen that file.

"The police have already questioned me about this," she admitted. "They agreed that I was right to have had doubts about Brighton. I gave them the files I'd taken and they let me go. End of story."

"Not even close. What made you suspicious of Brighton?"

She almost refused to answer, but maybe he knew something about this, as well. Maybe the tables would be reversed and he could provide her with some answers.

"Someone was following me," she explained. "Then once, someone actually tried to kidnap me. After that incident, I went to the police and they found a miniature tracking device taped on the undercarriage of my car. By then, there were rumors that Brighton was being investigated for illegal adoptions and lots of other criminal activity."

He shrugged. "So why take the files?"

"I thought I was just taking *my* file. I wanted to make sure there were no…irregularities. I wanted to verify that they hadn't done anything that would ultimately harm my baby."

That earned her a flat look.

"And you know the other file that you took was mine," he tossed out there to her.

Because Mia didn't think it would do any good to deny it, she nodded. "I don't know how it got mixed in with mine."

"Don't you?"

Surprised with his increasingly icy accusations, she shook her head. "No. I don't."

"Did you read the file?" he demanded.

"I glanced at it, because I didn't know what it was at first. I thought it was part of my records."

He made a sound to indicate he didn't believe her. "I'll bet you did more than glance. But then, you already knew what was in it, didn't you? You're the reason that file was at Brighton."

Stunned, Mia stared at him. She hadn't expected him to say that. Nor did she know why he'd said it. "I don't know what you mean."

"Of course, you do. Five years ago, I was diagnosed with Hodgkin's lymphoma. I'm cured now, but because my treatment could have left me sterile, I decided to stockpile some semen. It was stored in Cryogen Labs, here in San Antonio. That file you took, the one tucked inside yours, was my file from Cryogen." He paused. "What I want to know is why you did it?"

Tired of the ambiguous questions, Mia threw out her hands. "Did what?"

He huffed as if he thought she were stonewalling him. But she wasn't. Mia had absolutely no idea what he was talking about.

"He's your nephew," he said, enunciating each syllable. "That's what you said right after I told you that you'd had a son. You said that because—"

"I was delirious." Her voice was so filled with breath that it hardly had sound.

"No. You said it because you thought it was true. You thought I was my brother. Therefore, you thought my brother had a nephew. And since he's my only sibling, there's only one conclusion I can draw from that."

Logan McGrath stared at the carrier seat. "Judging from what I've uncovered, the little boy that I delivered is my own son."

* * * * *

If Logan McGrath ever wants to get a chance at fatherhood, he'd have to protect the mother of his child at all costs.
Look for NEWBORN CONSPIRACY by Delores Fossen, available for a limited time in February 2008 from Harlequin Intrigue.

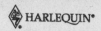

HARLEQUIN

1048

INTRIGUE

CASSIE MILES

MYSTERIOUS
MILLIONAIRE

Chapter One

Being a part-time private eye put a serious crimp in Liz Norton's social life. At half-past eleven on a Friday night in May, she ought to be wearing lip gloss, dancing, flirting and licking the suds off a beer that somebody else had paid for. Instead, she'd spent the past two hours and seventeen minutes on stakeout with Harry Schooner, her sixty-something boss.

She slouched behind the steering wheel of Harry's beat-up Chevy. Even with the windows cracked for ventilation, she still smelled stale hamburger buns from the crumpled bags littering the backseat. On the plus side, the cruddy, old car blended with the rundown Denver neighborhood where they were parked at the curb away from the streetlight, watching and waiting.

In the passenger seat, Harry pressed his fist against his chest and grunted.

"Are you okay?" she asked.

"Heartburn."

His digestive system provided a source of constant complaint. Long ago, she'd given up lecturing him on the evils of a strictly fast-food diet. "Did you take your pill?"

"What are you? My mother?"

"A concerned employee," she said. "If you keel over from a heart attack, where am I going to find another job as glamorous as this one?"

He peeled off the silver wrapping on a roll of antacid tablets, popped the last one in his mouth and tossed the wrapper over his shoulder into the trashed-out backseat. "That reminds me. You're done with your semester. Right?"

"Took my last exam two days ago."

At age twenty-six, she'd put herself halfway through law school. The accomplishment made her proud, even though she still heard echoes of her mother's refrain: *"Why bother with an education? The only way a girl like you can make it is to find a man to support you."* This bit of advice came right before the grooming tips: *"Lighten your hair, shorten your skirts and stand up straight so your boobs stick out."*

Of course, Liz did the exact opposite. Her thick, multi-colored blond hair remained undyed and unstyled— except for her own occasional hacking to keep the jagged ends near chin-length. Her wardrobe included exactly one skirt—knee-length and khaki—that she'd picked up at a thrift store for a buck. Mostly, she wore jeans and T-shirts. Tonight, a faded brown one under a black windbreaker. As for Mom's advice to show off her chest, Liz had given up on that plan long ago. Even if she arched her back like a pretzel, nobody would ever confuse her with a beauty queen.

Her twice-married mom had actually done her a favor when she'd shoved her only daughter out the door on her eighteenth birthday and told her that she was on her own.

Liz had done okay. Without a man.

Harry groaned again and shifted in the passenger seat. "You'll come to work for me full-time during your summer break. I could use the help. I'm getting too damn old for this job."

"Thanks, Harry." She'd been counting on this summer job. "But I still need Monday and Wednesday nights free to teach the under-twelve kids at the karate school."

"I got no problem with that." He made a wheezy noise through his nostrils and shrugged his heavy shoulders. His formerly athletic physique had settled into a doughy lump. Only his close-cropped white hair suggested the discipline of long-ago military service and twenty years as a cop. "How's my grandson doing at karate?"

"Not exactly a black belt, but he's hanging in there." She'd met Harry at Dragon Lou's Karate School when he'd come to watch his six-year-old grandson and ended up offering Liz a couple of part-time assignments.

Some aspects of being a P.I. were just plain nasty, like serving subpoenas or confirming the suspicions of a heartbroken wife about her cheating husband. But Liz enjoyed the occasional undercover disguise. Most of all, she liked grumpy old Harry and his two grown daughters. The Schooners represented the family she'd never had.

She peered through the scummy windshield at a ramshackle bungalow, landscaped with weeds and two rusty vehicles up on blocks. Gangsta music blared through the open windows. In the past hour, a half-dozen visitors had come and gone. She'd caught glimpses of three or four skinny children playing, even though it was way past normal bedtime, and she hoped the drug dealers inside the house weren't selling in front of the kids. Or to them.

"Are you sure we have the right address?"

"My source gave me the place, but not the time. He'll be here tonight." Harry rubbed his palms together. "Once we have photos of Mr. Crawford making a drug buy, we're in for a real big payday."

Liz found it hard to believe that Ben Crawford— millionaire adventurer and playboy—would show up in person. Didn't rich people hire underlings to do their dirty work?

But she hoped Harry was right. The Schooner Detective Agency could use the cash. They'd been retained by Ben's estranged wife, Victoria, who wanted enough dirt on her husband to void the prenup and gain sole custody of their five-year-old daughter. Photos of Ben making a drug buy would insure that Victoria got what she wanted, and she'd promised a huge bonus for the results.

Though Liz felt a twinge of regret about separating a father from his child, Ben Crawford deserved to be exposed. He'd been born with every advantage and was throwing his life away on drugs. In her book, that made him a lousy human being and definitely an unfit father.

A shiny, black Mustang glided to the curb in front of the house. This had to be their millionaire.

Harry shoved the camera into her hands. "You take the pictures. Don't worry. I'll back you up."

"Stay in the car, Harry."

"Get close to the front window," he said as he flipped open the glove compartment and took out an ancient Remington automatic.

A jolt of adrenaline turned her stakeout lethargy to tension. If Harry started waving his gun, this situation could get ugly. "Put that thing away."

"Don't you worry, Missy. I don't plan to shoot anybody." With another grunt, he opened his car door. "Go for the money shot. Crawford with the drugs in his hand."

The camera was foolproof—geared to automatically focus and adjust to minimal lighting. But she doubted she'd get a chance to use it. Most of the visitors to the house went inside, did their business and came out with hands shoved deeply into their pockets.

She darted across the street toward the dealer's house and ducked behind one of the junker cars in the driveway. Ben Crawford stood at the front door beside a bare bulb porch light. His shaggy brown hair fell over the collar of his worn denim shirt, only a few shades lighter than his jeans. He looked like a tall, rangy cowboy who had somehow gotten lost in the big city.

Holding the camera to her eye, Liz zoomed in on his face. *Wow.* Not only rich but incredibly good-looking, he had a firm jaw, high cheekbones and deep-set eyes. What was he doing here?

She pulled back on the zoom to include the dealer in his black mesh T-shirt and striped track pants. He pushed open the torn screen door and stepped onto the concrete slab porch under a rusted metal awning.

The pounding beat of rap music covered any noise Liz made as she clicked off several photos to make sure she caught them together.

Instead of going inside, Ben remained on the porch. For a moment, she hoped he wasn't here to make a buy, that there was a legitimate reason. Then he pulled a roll of bills from his pocket. The dealer handed over three brown, plastic vials.

Click. Click. Click. She had the money shot. A big payday for the Schooner Detective Agency.

The two men shook hands. Ben pivoted and returned to his Mustang while the dealer stood on the porch and watched Ben's taillights as he drove away.

Another man with a scraggly beard staggered outside and pointed.

Liz glanced over her shoulder to see what they were looking at. Harry crouched between two cars at the curb, his white hair gleaming in the moonlight.

"Hey, old man." The dealer came off the porch. "What the hell you doing?"

Harry straightened his stiff joints. "Guess I got lost."

"You watching us?" The two men stepped into the yard. From down the street, she heard ferocious barking, the prelude to a fight, and she knew Harry wasn't up to it.

She stashed the camera in the pocket of her windbreaker and rushed toward her partner. "There you are, Gramps. I've been looking all over for you." To the two men in the yard, she said, "Sorry if he bothered you. He wanders sometimes."

Their cold sneers told her that they weren't buying her story. The dealer snapped, "Stop right there, bitch."

"I'll just take Gramps home and—"

The crack of a gunshot brought her to a halt. She froze at the edge of the yard, praying that Harry wouldn't return fire. A shootout wouldn't be good for anybody.

Liz turned and faced the two men, who swaggered toward her. Her pulse raced, not so much from fear as uncertainty. She didn't know what to expect. Forcing an innocent smile, she said, "There's no need for guns."

"What's in your pocket? You carrying heat?"

As long as they didn't immobilize her, she ought to be able to take these two guys. Her five years studying martial arts at Dragon Lou's gave her an edge. Liz was capable of shattering a cinderblock with her bare hand.

From across the street, Harry yelled, "Leave her alone."

Please, Harry. Please don't use your gun. She had to act fast. No time to wait and see.

Liz aimed a flying kick at the bearded guy, neatly disarming him. Before his buddy could react, she whirled, chopped at his arm and kicked again. Though her hand missed, the heavy sole of her boot connected with his knee, and he stumbled.

The bearded man grabbed her forearm. Worst possible scenario. Both men had more brute strength than she did. Her advantage was speed and agility. She twisted and flipped, wrenching her arm free. He still clung to the sleeve of her windbreaker. She escaped by slipping out of her jacket.

Before they could brace themselves for another assault, she unleashed a series of kicks and straight-hand chops. Not a pretty, precise display. She wouldn't win any tournament points for style, but she got the job done with several swift blows to vulnerable parts of their anatomy. Throat. Gut. Groin.

Both were on their knees.

Another man rushed out the door. And another.

Behind her back, she heard Harry fire his automatic. Five shots.

She ran for the car.

Harry collapsed into the passenger side as she dived behind the wheel and cranked the ignition. Without turning on the headlights, she burned rubber and tore down the street.

Gunfire exploded behind them.

Liz didn't cut her speed until they reached a major intersection, where she turned on the headlights and merged into traffic. Her heart hammered inside her rib cage. They could have been killed. The aftermath of intense danger exploded behind her eyelids like belated fireworks.

Thank God for Dragon Lou and his martial arts training.

Beside her in the passenger seat, Harry was breathing heavily. With the back of his hand, he wiped sweat from his forehead. "Did you get the pictures?"

She cringed. "The camera was in my windbreaker. The bearded guy pulled it off me."

"It's okay."

"But you're not." She took note of his pasty complexion and heaving chest. "I'm taking you to the emergency room."

"You'd like that, wouldn't you? Kick the old man out of the way and take over his business."

"Yeah, that's my evil plan. Adding your debt to my student loans." Sarcasm covered her concern for him. "That's every girl's dream."

"Seriously, Liz. I don't need a doc." He exhaled in a long *whoosh* that dissolved into a hacking cough. "This was a little too much excitement for the old ticker."

"Is this your way of telling me that you have heart problems?"

"Forget it. Just drive back to the office."

Checking her rearview mirrors, she continued along Colfax Avenue. She didn't see anyone following them; they'd made a clean getaway. Just in case, she turned south at the next intersection and drove toward the highway. "We need to call the police."

"Nope."

"Harry, those guys shot at us. They assaulted us."

"But I returned fire." He cleared his throat, breathing more easily. His clenched fist lifted from his chest. "And you kicked ass. You might look like a Pop-Tart, but you were a fire-breathing dragon."

"My form wasn't terrific."

"You did good." He reached over and patted her shoulder. Always stingy with his compliments, Harry followed up with a complaint. "Too bad you messed up and lost the camera."

"Don't even think about taking the cost out of my wages." At a stoplight, she studied him again. He seemed to have recovered. "We need to fill out a police report. Those people are dealing drugs."

"And I guarantee that the narcs are well aware. Leave the drug dealers to the cops, we've got problems of our own. Like how to get that juicy bonus from Victoria."

Tomorrow, she'd put in a call to a friend at the Denver PD. At the very least, she wanted to see those children removed from a dangerous environment.

Harry sat up straighter. "Time to switch to Plan B."

"I don't like the sound of this."

"My source is the housekeeper who works at the Crawford estate near Evergreen. She can—"

"Wait a sec. How did you get to know a housekeeper?" She glanced toward the backseat. "You've never tidied up anything in your whole life."

"I served with her dad in Vietnam, and we stay in touch. Her name is Rachel Frakes. She's actually the one who recommended me to Victoria."

That connection explained a lot. The Schooner Detective Agency wasn't usually the first choice of the rich and famous. "What's Plan B?"

"Rachel gets you inside the estate. While you're there, you dig up the dirt on Ben."

"An undercover assignment."

That didn't sound too shabby. Maybe she'd impersonate a fancy-pants interior decorator. Or a horse wrangler. An upscale estate near Evergreen had to have several acres and a stable. Or she could be a guest—maybe an eccentric jet-setting heiress. A descendant of the Romanov czars. "Who am I supposed to be?"

He almost smiled. "You'll see."

Chapter Two

The next afternoon, Liz tromped down the back staircase from her brand-new undercover home—a third-floor garret at the Crawford mansion. Her starched gray uniform with the white apron reminded her of a Pilgrim costume she'd worn in fourth grade. The hem drooped below her knees, which was probably a good thing because she belatedly realized that she hadn't shaved her legs since before she started studying for final exams. Entering the kitchen, she adjusted the starched white cap that clung with four bobby pins to her unruly blond hair.

A maid. She was supposed to be a maid. The thrills just kept coming.

At the bottom of the staircase, Rachel the housekeeper stood with fists planted on her hips. She was a tall, solidly built woman who would have fit right in with the Russian women's weightlifting team. Her short blond hair was neatly slicked back away from her face. "Liz, may I remind you that a maid is supposed to be as unobtrusive as a piece of furniture."

"Okay." *Call me Chippendale.*

"While descending the staircase, you sounded like a herd of bison. We walk softly on the pads of our feet."

"If I walk softly, can I carry a big stick?"

Rachel's eyebrows shot up to her hairline. "Surely, you don't intend to hit anything."

"I'm joking." If this had been a real job, Liz would have already quit. "Any other advice?"

"The proper answer to a question is yes or no. Not 'okay.' And certainly not a joke. Is that clear?"

Liz poked at her silly white cap. "Yes, ma'am."

"Do something with your hair. It's all over the place."

She bit the inside of her mouth. "Yes, ma'am."

"No perfume. No nail polish. No makeup."

"No problem." That part of the assignment suited her normal procedure. "You know, Rachel, Harry and I really appreciate this—"

"Say nothing more." She pulled the door to the stairwell closed, making sure they were alone. "If anyone finds out what you're doing here, I'll deny any knowledge of your true profession."

"Yes, ma'am." In a low voice, she asked, "What can you tell me about Ben?"

"A fine-looking man but brooding. When Victoria told me about his drug problem, I had to act. I can't stand the thought of his daughter being raised by an addict."

"He doesn't usually live here, does he?"

"His home is in Seattle where he runs Crawford Aero-Equipment. They supply parts to the big airplane manufacturers and also build small custom jets."

Seemed like an extremely responsible job for a drug addict. "Why is he in Colorado?"

"This is his grandfather's house. Jerod Crawford." Her forehead pinched. "Jerod is a generous, brave man. He's dying from a brain tumor."

"And his grandson came home to take care of him."

Again, Ben's behavior wasn't what she'd expect from a druggie degenerate. Maybe he was here to make sure he inherited big bucks when grandpa died.

"For right now, you're needed in the kitchen," Rachel said. "We have a dinner party for sixteen scheduled for this evening."

Maybe some of these guests would provide negative evidence she could use against Ben. "Anybody I should watch for?"

"In what sense?"

"Other drug users. He must have gotten the name of his dealer from somebody."

"That's for you to investigate," Rachel said. "In the meantime, report to the kitchen."

"I'll be there in a flash. Right after I comb my hair."

Liz tiptoed up the stairs to the second floor. No matter what Rachel thought, her first order of business was to locate Ben's bedroom and search for his drug stash. She opened the door and stepped into the center of a long hallway decorated with oil paintings of landscapes. She peeked into an open door and saw an attractive bedroom with rustic furnishings—nothing opulent but a hundred times better than the tiny garret on the third floor where she'd dropped off her backpack and changed into the starchy maid outfit.

A tall brunette in a black pantsuit emerged from one of the rooms and stalked down the hallway.

Though Liz beamed a friendly smile, the brunette went past her without acknowledging her presence. Apparently, this was what it felt like to be furniture.

"Excuse me," Liz piped up.

The woman paused. "What?"

"I'm new here. And I'm looking for Ben's bedroom."

"My brother's room is right down there. Close to Grandpa."

The double doors to Jerod's room were open, and she heard other people inside. "Thank you."

There were too many people milling around to make a thorough search of Ben's room. Later, she'd come back. And right now? Liz wasn't anxious to report for maid duty in the kitchen. She'd use this time to explore, to get a sense of this sprawling house and the acreage that surrounded it.

Liz went down a short hallway beside the staircase. A beveled glass door opened onto the second-story outdoor walkway made of wood planks. At the far end, the walkway opened onto a huge, sunlit deck.

Towering pines edged up to the railing. Hummingbird feeders and birdhouses hung from the branches. Several padded, redwood chairs and chaises faced outward to enjoy the view, but no one was outside. Floor-to-ceiling windows lined this side of the house, which was very likely Jerod Crawford's bedroom. Lucky for her, the drapes were closed.

As Liz walked to the railing, a fresh mountain breeze

caressed her cheeks. Twitters from chipmunks and birds serenaded her. Multicolored petunias in attached wooden flower boxes bobbed cheerfully.

People like her didn't live in places like this. A grassy field dotted with scarlet Indian paintbrush and daisies rolled downhill, past a barn and another outbuilding, to a shimmering blue lake, surrounded by pines. In the distance, snow-covered peaks formed a majestic skyline.

At the edge of the lake, a wood dock stretched into the water. Though she was over a hundred yards away, she thought she recognized Ben. He faced a woman with platinum-blond hair and a bright red sweater.

Though Liz couldn't hear their words, they were obviously arguing. The woman gestured angrily. Ben pulled back as though he couldn't stand being close to her.

And then, she slapped him.

BEN RESTRAINED AN URGE to strike back at Charlene. Much as she had earned the right to have herthrown off his grandpa's property, that wasn't Ben's call.

Through tight lips, he said, "You're not always going to have things your way."

"No matter what you think, I'm the one in charge around here. Me. I'm Jerod's wife."

A ridiculous but undeniably true statement. At age thirty-six, she was only two years older than Ben himself. He hated having to consult with her on his grandpa's medical care and would never understand why the old man listened to her.

"Be reasonable, Charlene. I've been talking to specialists and neurosurgeons. They think Jerod's tumor could be removed."

"I don't want your doctors." She screeched like a harpy. "Jerod is happy with Dr. Mancini. And so am I."

Dr. Al Mancini had been the Crawford family doctor for years, and he was competent to treat sniffles and scraped knees. But a brain tumor? "Mancini isn't even practicing anymore. He's retired."

"And Jerod is his only patient. Dr. Mancini comes here every single day. Your specialist would put Jerod in the hospital. And he refuses."

- Unfortunately, Charlene was correct. His stubborn, Texas-born grandpa had planted himself here and wouldn't budge. Every day, the tumor inside his head continued to grow. His vision was seriously impaired, and he barely had the strength to get out of his wheelchair. "If not an operation, he needs access to other treatments. Radiation. Cutting-edge medications."

"He won't go. And I'm not going to force him."

For the moment, he abandoned this topic. There were other bones to pick. "At least, cancel your damn dinner party. Jerod needs peace and quiet."

"You want to pretend like he's already dead. Well, he's not. He needs activity and excitement. That's why he married me."

"Really? I thought it had more to do with your thirty-six double-D chest."

She slapped him again. This time, he'd earned it.

With a swish of her hips, Charlene flounced up the hill toward the house.

Five years ago, when his grandpa had announced that he wanted to marry a Las Vegas showgirl, Ben had been almost proud of the old guy. After a lifetime of hard work in the Texas oil fields, Jerod had the right to amuse himself. Even if it meant the rest of the family had to put up with a gold digger.

Charlene had readily agreed to a very generous pre-nuptial agreement. Whether their marriage was ended by divorce or death, she walked away with a cool half million in cash. Not a bad deal.

Ben had expected Charlene to divorce his grandpa after a year and grab the cash, but she'd stayed…and stayed…and stayed. In her shallow way, she might even love Jerod. And he had to admit that their May–December marriage had turned out better than his. Nothing good had come from that union, except for his daughter.

He walked to the end of the small dock. A spring wind rippled the waters. Trout were jumping. In the rolling foothills of Colorado, he saw the swells of the ocean. He missed his home in Seattle that overlooked the sea, but he cherished every moment here with his grandpa as the old man prepared for his final voyage.

Behind his back, Ben heard someone step onto the dock. He turned and saw a gray maid's uniform. "What is it?"

"You must be Ben." She marched toward him with her hand outthrust. "I'm Liz Norton. The new maid."

He accepted her handshake. Though she was a slender little thing, her grip was strong. He took a second look at her. The expression in her luminous green eyes showed a surprising challenge. Not the usual demeanor for household staff. "Is this your first job as a servant?"

"Servant?" Her nose wrinkled in disgust. "I can't say that I like that job description. Sounds like I ought to curtsey."

"I suppose you have a more politically correct job title in mind."

She pulled her hand away from his grasp and thought for half a second. "Housekeeping engineer."

In spite of her droopy gray uniform, she radiated electricity, which might explain why her hair looked like she'd stuck her finger in a wall socket. He would have dismissed her as being too cute. Except for the sharp intelligence in her green eyes.

"Nice place you've got here." She stepped up beside him. "Are there horses?"

"Not anymore. Horses were my grandmother's passion. Arabians. God, they were beautiful." He had fond memories of grooming the horses with his grandmother. "After she passed away, ten years ago, Jerod sold them to someone who would love them as much as she had."

"Wise decision. Every living creature needs to be with someone who loves them."

A hell of a profound statement. "Are you? With someone who loves you?"

"I do okay." She cocked her head and looked up at him. "How about you, Ben? Who loves you?"

"My daughter," he responded quickly. "Natalie."

Her expression went blank as if she had something to

hide. All of a sudden, her adorable freckled face seemed less innocent. He wondered why she'd approached him, why she spoke of love.

There had been incidents in the past when female employees had tried to seduce him, but Liz's body language wasn't flirtatious. Her arms hung loosely at her sides. Her feet were planted solidly. Something else motivated her.

"You have a reputation as an adventurer," she said. "What kind of stuff do you do? Something with the airplanes you manufacture?"

"I test-pilot our planes. Not for adventure. It's work."

She arched an eyebrow. "Cool job."

"I'm not complaining." He glanced up the hill toward the house. It was time to get his grandpa outside in the sun. Maybe he could talk some sense into the old man. "Please excuse me, Liz."

Instead of stepping politely aside, she stayed beside him, matching her gait to his stride. "I think I met your sister at the house. Real slim. Dressed in black."

"That's Patrice." And *not* good news. He'd known that his sister and her husband, Monte, were coming to dinner, but he hadn't expected her until later. As a rule, he tried to keep his sister and Charlene separate. The two women hated each other.

"Is your sister married?" Liz asked.

"Yes."

"Any kids?"

Patrice was far too selfish to spoil her rail-thin figure by getting pregnant. "None."

From the house, he heard a high-pitched scream.

Ben took off running.

When he looked over, he saw Liz with her uniform hiked up, racing along beside him. She had to be the most unusual maid he'd ever met.

* * * * *

The maid and the millionaire join forces to keep his young daughter alive while a killer prowls the darkest corners of the mansion....
Look for MYSTERIOUS MILLIONAIRE by Cassie Miles, available for a limited time in March 2008 from Harlequin Intrigue.

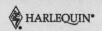

HARLEQUIN®

INTRIGUE®

HARLEQUIN INTRIGUE IS THE PERFECT
COMBINATION OF PASSIONATE ROMANCE
AND NONSTOP SUSPENSE.

On sale March 2008

Available wherever
books are sold, including
most bookstores,
supermarkets, drugstores
and discount stores.

Receive $1.00 off

MYSTERIOUS MILLIONAIRE

**or any other
Harlequin Intrigue novel.**

Coupon expires August 1, 2008.
Redeemable at participating retail outlets in the U.S. only.
Limit one coupon per customer.

5 65373 00076 2   (8100) 0 11479

HI08COUP3R

ANN VOSS PETERSON

THRILLER

WYOMING MANHUNT

Chapter One

Shanna felt the sound of the gunshot more than she heard it. The first sharp report jangled her nerves. The second cracked through her ear and jaw, so close she could almost feel the air stirred by the bullet. She released her mare's reins and threw her body to the ground. She hit dirt, neck snapping to the side, air exploding from her lungs. Her horse's hooves pounded the dry earth, the sound fading into the distance.

What had just happened?

Shanna raised her head. Dry brown grass swayed in front of her, sparkling with frost. White caps of mountains rose all around her. Silence hung heavy in the morning air.

Obviously someone in her hunting party had seen deer and taken a shot…and she'd let the sound scare the sense out of her.

Her cheeks heated. She'd told Mr. Barstow she was no hunter, but this would make her the laughingstock of not only her hunting party, but also all of Talbot Mining. She could hear her friend Linda's giggle now.

Shaking her head at her own ridiculousness, Shanna stifled a laugh and struggled to her feet. As long as her overreaction to the first rifle shot didn't lose her a promotion, she would laugh along. No one could say Shanna Clarke wasn't a good sport.

Brushing her gloved hands over her orange jacket and insulated pants, she peered in the direction of her fleeing horse. The mare had reached the outfitter's pack mules. The other three members of the hunting party gathered several yards away. Mr. Barstow, the CEO of Talbot, stood on the ground. Behind him, Ron Davis, the chief financial officer, and Sheriff Gable remained astride their horses. Mr. Barstow raised his rifle to his shoulder and took aim.

At her.

She fell back to the ground. Didn't he see her? She glanced around, expecting to see a mule deer behind her, hoping to see…

Nothing was there.

Panic slammed against her ribs. Her lungs seized, making it hard to breathe. She had to be mistaken.

She raised her head, peering over the long grass once again.

Her boss's rifle was trained on her.

She ducked before the shot cracked through the air. Her heart slammed against her ribs. Barstow was shooting at her. *Shooting at her.*

Her head swirled. It didn't make sense. None of it made sense.

She tried to rise, tried to move, but her legs were too

weak to support her. She had to get out of here. For her little Emily's sake. For her own sake. She didn't want to die.

Forcing herself to her hands and knees, she started to crawl, moving through the tufted, brown grass. If she remembered correctly, there was a rocky slope in this direction. Once she started down the slope, Barstow wouldn't be able to see her.

At least until he caught up.

The frozen earth was hard under her knees and hands. Her breath rasped in her throat, making it impossible to hear anything else. She imagined the sound of hooves, pounding across the valley faster than she could ever hope to move. They'd catch up to her in no time.

The ground grew rockier, digging through thick pants and gloves. She tried to move faster, waiting for the pounding hooves, waiting for the crack of gunfire, the impact of the bullet.

A report shattered the air.

Gasping, she glanced behind. Nothing but dry grass moved behind her. She forced herself to keep crawling.

The ground sloped downward. Gray rock replaced the waving grass. Shanna scrambled to her feet, forcing her legs to work. Crouching low, she stumbled over rock. Boots slipping and skidding, she picked her way down the slope.

Another crack split the air.

She glanced behind, expecting to see horses on the edge of the slope, a rifle barrel pointed at her, but they hadn't reached her. Not yet.

The ground fell out from under her feet.

She rolled and stumbled, trying to right herself. Scrub brush scraped at her face, ripped at her coat. Jumbled sound filled her head. She landed on her hands. Pain shuddered up her arms. She pitched forward onto a shelf of rock.

Shanna gasped. Pain stabbed through her neck.

Gritting her teeth, she rolled to her side and struggled to her knees. Her neck screamed. Her legs felt boneless. She forced herself to move, scrambling along the shelf. The rock above tongued outward, creating an overhang. She slipped underneath. Lying on her side, she curled her back into the crevice and pulled her legs in tight.

She could hear them now. The beats of hooves. Or maybe it was her imagination. It didn't matter. She couldn't check. If she peeked out from under the rock, they'd surely see her.

"Shanna?"

She tensed at the gruff sound of her boss's voice. So it wasn't her imagination. He was there. At the top of the ridge? Or closer? She held her breath.

"I'm sorry I scared you, Shanna. I didn't see you. I wouldn't have fired if I knew you were down range. It was an accident."

An accident? She tried to replay what had happened in her mind. The sound of the shots. The sight of Barstow lining up for shot number two. Could it have been an accident?

"Come on, Shanna. You can't think I was *trying* to shoot you."

Did she think that? Yes, she had. As soon as she saw that rifle barrel she'd thought exactly that. But what possible reason could Mr. Barstow have for wanting her dead?

"You're not hurt, are you?"

He sounded worried. Shanna tightened her grip on her legs, hugging them close. She wanted it all to be a mistake. She wanted Mr. Barstow to be telling the truth, to be worried that she was hurt. But was he really? How could she have gotten everything so wrong?

"Shanna? Talk to me, honey. Tell me you're all right. Please? Shanna?"

She opened her mouth and drew in a breath. But she couldn't get the image of him raising the gun out of her head. She closed her mouth and pressed her lips tightly together.

"Make a sound so I know where you are. I'll get the others and we'll come down for you."

She wanted to call out. Her throat ached with it. She needed to make this nightmare go away.

The broken hiss of a whisper rode across the wind, too faint for her to catch the words.

Unease prickled all the way up her spine. It was Barstow. She was sure of it. Even in a whisper, she could recognize that commanding, gruff voice. He must be talking to someone. One of the others from the hunting party. But why whisper?

Because he didn't want her to hear.

She stifled the whimper struggling to break from her lips. She had no more time to think. No time to wish things were different. If she wanted to get out of this alive, if she wanted to see her little girl again, she had to move. And she had to do it now.

She tilted her head back. Pain shot through her neck. Sucking in a sharp breath, she blinked the tears from her eyes and tried to take in her surroundings. The shelf of rock stretched at least a hundred yards. If she moved carefully and quietly, maybe she could shuffle her body under the shelf. Maybe she could put some distance between her and the men without them seeing. Maybe she could get away before they found her.

She had to.

Chapter Two

A crash sounded from up the slope. Jace Lantry glanced up from the long, clawed footprint in the patch of snow and scanned the rough terrain that rose behind his ranch. Something was running through pine and fir. Maybe the grizzly that left this footprint. Or its prey.

Tilting his hat low, he squinted at the trees, the wide brim shielding his eyes from the morning sun. He didn't have anything against the bears. Hell, the land was theirs long before humans moved in. They'd never messed with his livestock. Grizzlies rarely did. They ate plants, most of the time. But he'd better make sure the fortress he built around his garbage cans would hold. The last thing he wanted was a momma grizzly deciding his cabin would make a nice restaurant. If that happened, there was no telling what she'd assume was on the menu.

A flash of blaze orange bobbed through the clump of trees.

Not bear. Hunter.

Oh, hell. When Jace had agreed to lease land to his neighbor for hunting season, he'd specified Roger could only use acreage east of Gusset Ridge. This wasn't the first time this season that a wealthy hunter had wandered past the cutoff point and gotten himself lost. Roger might be a good outfitter, but he was awful when it came to controlling his rich clients. The guy was too damn nice.

Fortunately Jace didn't have any qualms about laying down the law to a straying hunter. He'd bought this ranch in the Wyoming wilderness so he'd never have to look out for anyone but himself again. The last thing he was going to do was provide some kind of hand-holding to a wealthy SOB who didn't think he had to follow the rules.

Wait a second.

The hunter broke from the cover of Engelmann spruce and ran along the forest's edge. Shoulder-length blond hair peeked from under the orange stocking cap. The unmistakable curve of a woman's hip was evident under the boxy orange coat. She stumbled through the dry grass and occasional patch of snow, no rifle, no concern for frightening her game. In fact, *she* looked like the frightened one.

The crack of rifle fire reverberated through the trees.

The woman ducked. Slipping, she fell to her knees. Thrusting herself back to her feet, she zigged through the edge of the forest, as if certain the gunshot had been meant for her.

Something wasn't right. Not right at all. He didn't have to have been a cop in his previous life in order to figure that out. And judging from the woman's present course, she was running straight for his homestead.

Jace groaned out loud.

An eye on the woman, he headed for his cabin. He'd moved to the mountains to escape trouble. But it appeared she had found him anyway.

SHANNA CROSSED the open slope, running flat out for the small log cabin and outbuildings nestled along a stream. Her boots skidded in a patch of snow. Her breath rasped in her throat, making her ears ache almost as much as her head and neck.

Crawling under the rock shelf and the rough terrain of the slope had given her a head start against the mounted men. But that last crack of gunfire proved Barstow was still on her heels. And it wouldn't take him long to figure out where she was headed.

She had to pray she could find someone to help her, a vehicle she could borrow, or at least a place to hide.

The cabin was closest, separated from the other buildings by split-rail fencing. Maybe the place had a phone.

She reached the cabin. She sidled up to a mullioned window and peered inside. The place was rustic and simple, with the kitchen, dining area and living room all visible from the side window. She didn't see anyone inside.

She also didn't see a phone.

She closed her eyes for a moment and forced herself to take a long breath. She might be able to break in to a simple little cabin like this. But if there was no phone, that wouldn't get her very far. When she thought about it, she had no clue who to call anyway. The sheriff was with Barstow. He'd watched while her boss had lined up his shot.

She had to get out of here, and she had to do it now.

She scanned the distance to the other buildings. A pole barn dominated the ranch, surrounded by a fence. Past the corrals and next to the barn, dirt ruts led into a square structure.

A garage?

She peeked into the cabin again, this time scanning countertops and the area around the front door for anything that looked like car keys. Nothing. But maybe that was a good sign. Maybe whoever owned this place kept his keys in the garage.

Giving the rocky slope behind the cabin a glance, she ran for the garage. She reached the first fence. She stepped over the lowest rail and ducked under the second. Sharp pain shot down her neck. She ignored it and pushed on. If Barstow caught her, a sore neck would be the least of her worries.

She ran across the corral's bare dirt, struggling to hear over her breath rasping in her throat, her heartbeat pounding in her ears. Horses looked up from the round bale they munched on. One spooked and darted through an open gate and into the larger field beyond.

Her nerves stretched taut. She tried to run faster. She had no cover. If Barstow and the others cleared the evergreens while she was still crossing to the garage, she was done for. They wouldn't have any trouble hitting her with their high-powered rifles.

She reached the other side of the fenced pen and

ducked under and out. She raced to the garage. Grabbing the doorknob, she held her breath and twisted.

It turned under her hand.

She pushed the door open and slipped inside, leaving the door open a crack behind her.

The garage was dark, but with the door cracked, not too dark to see a hulking shadow parked in its center. A truck. A way out. She just had to find a key.

She strained her eyes in the dim light and groped the wall around the door, hoping to find a key hook or nail. Nothing but studs and steel. She crossed to the truck and opened the driver's door. Light shone from the cab. Fear thickening in her throat, she used the extra light to quickly scan the area for any sign of keys. Coming up empty, she climbed into the pickup's cab and closed the door.

Plunged back into darkness, she willed her eyes to adjust. She felt for a key in the ignition switch, then groped under the floor mat. Nothing. Where else might someone hide a car key? She slipped a hand between sun visor and roof.

Her fingers hit metal.

A whimper catching in her throat, she grasped the key. She tried to keep her hand steady, tried to fit key into switch.

The passenger door jerked open. Light flared all around her.

"What the hell do you think you're doing?"

Her whimper turned into a gasp as she looked into the barrel of a shotgun.

JACE WAITED FOR some kind of sound to come out of the woman's open lips. Her throat moved, but not so much as a squeak broke the silence. Hell. Looked like he'd have to help her out. "Trying to steal my truck?"

"No. I mean…" She looked down at her hand, as if just realizing she held the key. She looked back at him with a pair of the biggest green eyes he'd ever seen. "I'm sorry…I didn't… I had to… Please, don't shoot." She raised her hands in the air.

Double hell. He canted the barrel to the side. Why he should feel guilt over frightening a car thief, he didn't know. But one look at those wide eyes, those trembling lips, and the need to rush in like some sort of damn savior pulled at him like a physical force. Once a cop, always a cop, he supposed. "You can put your hands down."

She did.

"Okay, start by telling me what's going on. I don't want to shoot you. But it looks like not everyone feels the same."

She took in a shuddering breath. "My boss."

"Your boss?"

"He's trying to shoot me."

That was a new definition for the term *boss from hell.* "Why?"

She shook her head. "I don't know."

Hard to believe. It was always the same. Under interrogation, every criminal was completely innocent. Every scumbag a victim through no fault of his own. "You sure about that?"

Tears welled in her eyes. She raised her hands in front

of her, as if totally at a loss. "I don't know what's going on. I swear. I thought I was up for a promotion."

Talk about not reading the signs...

Jace bit back the quip. As surreal as this whole situation seemed, it wasn't the time for jokes. If someone was gunning for this woman, he didn't want to get in front of the bullet. As a cop, he'd gone ten years without ever firing his gun. And he'd never been shot, either. He didn't plan for that to change now that he was no longer on the job.

Let the guys who *hadn't* been kicked off the force handle it. "I'll call the sheriff."

Panic streaked across her face. "No! You can't!"

He felt a tightening in his gut. He knew there was more to this. He could feel it. "Why not?"

"The sheriff. He's with them."

"He wants to kill you, too?" That was even harder to buy than the boss's sudden homicidal urge. "This keeps getting better and better."

"You've got to believe me."

He didn't *have* to do anything. "Why is the sheriff after you?"

"I don't know."

He had a guess. "You break the law?"

"No. I told you. I thought I was getting a promotion."

He let out a heavy sigh.

"I'm telling you the truth. We were supposed to be hunting deer, and my boss started shooting at me."

"And the sheriff? How does he fit in?"

"He was there. Just standing there watching."

"Are you sure it wasn't an accident? Are you sure he wasn't shooting at, say, a deer?"

Redness rimmed her eyes, as if she were about to burst into tears at any moment. "I'm sure. He came after me. He's chasing me. The others are, too."

"The others, meaning, the sheriff."

She nodded. "And the CFO of the company where I work."

This was ludicrous. He shouldn't believe her. But he'd seen her running along the line of trees. And God help him, she seemed scared out of her wits. "So what do you expect me to do? Stand out front and return fire?"

For a moment she looked at him as if that was exactly what she was thinking. She shook her head. "Of course not."

"What then?"

"Just lend me your truck. I'll return it. I promise."

He almost laughed. "You must think I'm an idiot."

She shook her head. "I know it sounds bad. But I'll return it. I swear, I will. I have to get out of here."

Movement caught his eye through the opening in the door. He held up a hand.

The woman gasped. She covered her mouth with trembling fingers.

Jace felt the weight of the shotgun. The last thing he wanted to do was get in some sort of old-west shootout. But what could he do? He might not believe everything this woman was saying, but that didn't mean he could just hand her over to people who might want to kill her and wash his hands of the whole thing. He might no longer be part of law enforcement, but he was still a cop where it counted. A true cop. At least he liked to think so.

He held out his hand, palm up. "The key."

She dropped the truck's ignition key into his hand.

"Get in the backseat and crouch down on the floor. There's a blanket back there you can use to cover yourself."

"Thank you."

He didn't know what to think about this woman. He sure didn't buy her ridiculous story. Not without some kind of evidence to back it up. "Don't thank me yet."

He stuffed the truck's ignition key in his jeans pocket. Turning toward the door, he held the shotgun at the ready, took a deep breath and willed the spot running from the center of his chest to the waistband of his jeans to stop jittering.

Here went nothing.

He strode out of the garage. The brightness of the sun stunned him for a moment. Tilting his hat low over his eyes, he scanned the house, the barn, the corrals.

A heavyset man circled the fence line. Dressed in a bright orange coat and sporting a gray cowboy hat on his head, he held his rifle as if he intended to use it.

Jace pushed a stream of air through tight lips. It fogged in the cool autumn air. "You looking for someone?"

The man started slightly, but kept walking forward. "You the landowner?" he called out in a loud voice.

"Yes. Jason Lantry."

"I'm Benson Gable, the sheriff around here."

Jace lowered his weapon. He pulled out his best

relaxed smile and plastered it to his face. "Nice to meet you, Sheriff. What can I do you for?"

The sheriff also lowered his gun and came to a stop two yards from Jace. "There's a fugitive in the area. Looks like she was headed to your ranch here."

"She?"

He gave a sharp nod. "Reddish blond hair. She's dressed in hunting garb. Orange coat, orange hat."

"Like you."

"Yes."

Jace had been hoping the sheriff would divulge a little more. Like something that proved the woman was lying. Something that would allow Jace to turn her in and walk away with a clear conscience. Well, if the sheriff wasn't going to come out with it, there was nothing wrong with asking. "What did she do?"

"Can't go in to that. But she's armed. And definitely dangerous. Mind if I take a look around?"

"I'd like to help you, Sheriff. I really would. But there's been no woman around this place for longer than I care to think about, and I have an appointment I really have to get to." He glanced at his watch for emphasis.

"You won't mind then if we look to make sure. She might have slipped in when you weren't looking."

"We?"

"I have a deputy circling the property."

The woman's boss? The chief financial officer? Or actual deputies? With his luck, one had already slipped into the garage, found the woman, and they were about to arrest him for being an accessory to whatever crime she'd committed. He'd land back in jail without even knowing what hit him.

He stifled the shudder that thought inspired. "Got a warrant?"

The sheriff shook his massive head. "Nah. Don't worry about that."

"I'd feel better if you tell me what she's wanted for."

The sheriff hitched up his pants. "Lover's spat. Shot her boyfriend."

Was it possible? Had the woman's terror been about being caught? Had she been feeding him a line of bull?

Jace didn't know. He couldn't shake the sight of her hitting the ground at the sound of the rifle shot. No sheriff he knew would take potshots at a fleeing suspect with a deer rifle. Not if he was on the up-and-up. "I'd feel better if you had a warrant."

"No need for a warrant, son. We don't suspect you of doing anything wrong."

"Happy to hear that."

He took a step forward. Looking past Jace, he eyed the garage.

"But you'll still need a warrant."

"What's your game, son?"

"No game. I just want to protect myself. I was on the job once. Had to have a warrant for every damn thing. I figure now that I'm on this end, there might be something to it."

The sheriff gave him a look that suggested he'd rather shoot him than show him a warrant. "Where you from?"

Meaning, where had he served as a cop. "Denver."

"Figures. Things aren't done that way around here. People trust the law." He narrowed his eyes and scanned the corrals and cabin beyond. "Unless you got something to hide. You got something to hide, Jason Lantry?"

Jace held up his hands, praying he wasn't getting himself in so deep he couldn't dig himself out. "Nothing to hide. If this woman did what you say, I'll be glad to truss her up and hand her over."

Again, the sheriff eyed the garage. "What's in there?"

"My truck."

"That where you came from just now?"

Jace nodded. "Like I said, I was getting ready to head out. I have an appointment."

The sheriff's cheeks puffed into a smile. "You want me to get a warrant? You know how it works. You're going to have to stay here and wait. No way you'll make your appointment."

Jace canted his head to the side, as if considering this. It was the perfect way out. If he wanted to take it. If he trusted the woman. If he wanted to stretch his neck between the guillotine blades.

Jace tried to keep his breathing even. He'd interrogated enough bad guys to know how good lying was done. But even after all his disappointments with the Denver P.D., the idea of not cooperating with the sheriff sat in his gut like a cold stone. A cop didn't obstruct an investigation. Especially not when the most compelling reason he had to believe the suspect was a set of pretty green eyes. "Okay. Can't say I see any harm in letting you look around."

The sheriff gave a satisfied nod. He glanced in the direction of Jace's cabin. "Back door is open. I suppose it's possible she could have slipped in there."

Jace followed his gaze just in time to see a man wearing hunting gear duck around the cabin's corner.

A man whose face he recognized.

Jace glanced back at the sheriff. "One of your deputies?"

The sheriff gave him a look as if to say, it's none of your damn business. "Yup."

Jace nodded. There was no hope for an easy way out of this now. He'd seen that man on the nightly news, and he was no sheriff's deputy. He was CEO of Wyoming's most successful state-based mining operation, Anthony Barstow…and quite possibly the woman's boss.

He raised a hand and waved to the sheriff. "Okay, then. I'm out of here. Good luck finding her." His voice sounded strained, gruff, and he could only hope the sheriff didn't notice.

He didn't seem to. Probably too busy with his own plans to make his rich friend happy by hunting down a woman with strawberry-blond hair and big green eyes.

Not willing to waste one more moment, Jace strode back to the garage. The quicker he got the hell out of here, the better.

Rounding the barn, he rolled up the garage door. He returned his shotgun to its rack near the garage door. He'd like to take it with him, under the circumstances. But he didn't need to risk breaking Wyoming gun laws by having a loaded gun in the truck. Just in case he was pulled over.

Of course, that might be the least of his troubles.

He climbed into his pickup. He didn't glance in the backseat or check the rearview mirror, but he knew she was there. He could smell the light scent of her, some kind of floral shampoo mixed with the metallic tang of fear. "Hold on, this is likely to be a bumpy ride."

UNDERSTATEMENT of the year.

Shanna clung to the floor of the truck, her stomach growing queasier by the moment as the truck bucked and bumped. It was a good thing she hadn't had much for breakfast, because she wouldn't have been able to keep it anyway.

"Here we go."

One big jolt and the truck rolled on comparatively smooth pavement.

She was safe for now.

* * * * *

On the run in the wilderness...a rancher and a single mother...and they're running out of time!
Look for WYOMING MANHUNT by Ann Voss Peterson, available for a limited time in March 2008 from Harlequin Intrigue.

INTRIGUE

HARLEQUIN
INTRIGUE

ELLE
JAMES

TEXAS-SIZED
SECRETS

Chapter One

> Wanted: Cowboy. Must be able to ride, rope and
> fence. Can't be afraid of hard work and long hours.
> Most of all, must know how to handle a gun.
> Position considered dangerous. See M. Grainger at
> the Rancho Linda.

The want ad sounded more like something out of the
Wild West, not the new millennium. Who the hell adver-
tised for a hired gun in this day and age? And how many
nutcases would come out of the hills in response?

Reed Bryson stared one last time at the crumpled
paper before he stepped down from his truck. Jobs were
scarce in Briscoe County. It wasn't as if he had a lot of
choices.

For the second time this year he was interviewing for
work. Although he'd gone thirteen years without riding a
horse, he knew he'd have no trouble. Roping would come
back, and moving cattle was as natural as breathing to him
despite the time lapse. He met all the requirements of the
job notice he'd picked up at Dee's Diner. Even the last one.

Twelve years on the Chicago police force had honed his ability to fire a gun and to know when.

A shiny white dually stood next to his truck with Teague Oil & Gas printed on the doors. He'd seen the vehicle in Prairie Rock over the past couple months. Oil speculators were as thick as horseflies in the panhandle.

He settled his Stetson on his head and strode to the two-story, white, wood frame house. It probably dated back to the nineteenth century, with its wide wraparound porches, tall windows and doors designed to catch the breeze. A place built for air movement back when air conditioners weren't yet invented.

The front door was open, with the screen door firmly in place to keep the pesky horseflies out.

When Reed raised his hand and knocked, two men in tailored business suits appeared in the doorway.

"We'll be back tomorrow same time. Hopefully, Grainger can meet with us then." They stepped through the screen, each running a narrow-eyed glance over Reed as they descended from the porch without so much as a howdy-do. They climbed into the pickup and drove off, leaving a trail of dust floating over the prairie grass.

Footsteps echoed in the foyer and a short, plump Hispanic woman smiled a greeting. *"Buenos días, señor."*

"Habla inglés?"

"Sí. I speak very good English. What can I do for you?" Her English was excellent and laced with a charming hint of Mexican accent. She opened the door and held it with her hip while she dried wet hands on her apron.

"I'm here to see Mr. Grainger about the job."

The woman's gaze followed the dually as it left. When the oilmen disappeared out of sight, she switched her perusal to him, her glance traveling from hat to boots before she spoke again. "Check with my husband down by the barn. He'll know where to find the boss."

"Thank you, ma'am."

"De nada."

As Reed rounded the corner of the house, he could feel the woman's gaze following him. He couldn't blame her. After the oil speculators' visit, he'd be cautious too, as he was with all salesmen.

The barn stood two hundred yards from the house. As Reed approached, a dark-haired, dark-skinned man led a bay mare out of the building. The man stopped as he cleared the doorway and turned to adjust the saddle girth beneath the horse's belly.

"Excuse me." Reed slowed as he approached.

The man looked up and nodded, but continued tightening the strap.

"I'm looking for Mr. Grainger. I'm here about the job."

The man's brows rose up his forehead. "I'm going there now. Saddle up, you can come along." He led Reed into the dark interior of the barn and stopped in front of the second stall. A black horse with a white star on his forehead leaned over the stall door. "You ride Diablo."

When Reed hesitated, the man smiled.

"Don't worry. His name is worse than his reputation." A chuckle echoed through the interior of the big barn.

"That's good to know."

The man held out a hand. "I'm Fernando Garcia, the

foreman." His words rolled off his tongue with the natural ease of one who'd grown up speaking Spanish as his first language.

"Reed Bryson." He clasped the man's hand in a firm handshake. Then he moved to the stall, holding out his fingers for the horse to sniff.

"Careful, amigo, he may not be a devil to ride, but he's been known to have a helluva bite."

Reed jerked his hand back and opened the stall door. He snagged the horse's halter and led him out into the center aisle.

Fernando tossed a blanket over the gelding's back and followed with a saddle. Reed quickly cinched the saddle in place and slid a bridle over the horse's head, slipping the bit between stubbornly clamped teeth.

Fernando nodded. "I'll wait outside. We need to hurry, it's getting close to dark and I haven't seen the boss in a couple hours."

Reed braced a boot in a stirrup and swung his right leg over the saddle. When he emerged into the waning sunlight, he blinked at the brightness after being in the dark interior of the barn.

As soon as Reed exited the barn, Fernando took off.

Reed pressed his heels into Diablo's flanks and the beast took off at a gallop. As if it hadn't been thirteen years since Reed had been on the back of a horse, he settled into the smooth rhythm. He urged his mount forward until he rode side by side with Fernando.

Galloping wasn't the best time to quiz the man, but Reed wanted to know more about the job before he committed to it—*if* the boss saw fit to hire him. "Has there been trouble on the ranch?"

"*Sí.*" The foreman either was in a big hurry or he wasn't sharing what kind of trouble. The older man nudged his horse faster, racing across the low range grasses of the Texas panhandle.

Knowing he wasn't getting any more information out of the man, Reed dropped back, content to follow. His questions would be answered soon enough by the ranch owner himself.

Fernando topped a rise and dropped down behind it.

When Reed reached the top of the slope, his heart leaped into his throat at the steep drop on the other side.

As if anxious to catch the other horse, Diablo danced to the side, straining against the reins.

"Okay, go for it." Reed gave the horse his head and held on while the animal plunged downward into a small canyon tangled with a maze of ravines and fallen rocks.

He thought he heard someone's shouts echoing off the canyon walls, but the sound of the horse's hooves slipping and sliding down the rocky path could have been playing tricks on his hearing.

Fernando had eased his horse into a walk, picking his way through the rocks and bramble that spooked his mount. With the skill of one born to ride, the man held his seat and urged his mount to continue down the hill to the bottom of the canyon.

A riderless horse passed Reed and leaped over the top of the hill behind him. He assumed it was the boss's horse and spurred his own forward at a lethal pace for the downhill slide.

When Reed reached the canyon floor, he just caught a glimpse of Fernando's horse rounding the corner of a sheer bluff wall.

Without hesitation, Reed dug his heels into the horse's flanks and raced after him, wondering, not for the first time, if this was some kind of test or trap. He reached beneath his denim jacket and flicked the safety strap off his Glock. Whether he was being led into an ambush or the boss of the Rancho Linda was really in trouble, he'd be ready.

When he rounded yet another corner of rocky wall, he pulled up sharply, narrowly avoiding a collision with Fernando and his mount.

Diablo reared and screamed.

Fernando's bay mare danced to the side but refused to go forward.

Ahead a hundred yards was a cow, lying on her side, clearly in the midst of a birthing gone bad. In front of her was a herd of wild hogs. Between the downed cow and the canyon wall stood a small woman with flowing black hair and brown-black eyes. She waved her straw cowboy hat at the angry animals and yelled. As small as she was, she wasn't making much of an impression on the three-hundred-pound swine circling her and the distressed cow.

Fernando pulled his rifle from the scabbard on the front of his saddle and aimed it in the air. A round exploded, the sound echoing off the canyon walls.

While most of the hogs jumped and scattered, a few

of the larger, more aggressive males turned their attention from the girl to Fernando. Fearless, or too mad to care, two of the beasts charged.

The older man's horse reared and spun. In order to stay in the saddle, Fernando had to drop the rifle and hold on. His horse lit out with several of the hogs in pursuit.

Reed's horse danced to the side behind a stand of rocks. A scream ripped across the canyon walls, chilling his blood.

The largest of the boars rammed into the cow's swollen belly. The cow bellowed and tried to roll to her feet. With a calf lodged in the birthing canal, she wasn't going anywhere.

The woman behind the cow shouted and waved her hat. "Get the hell away from her. Get!"

What did she hope to accomplish? Her little bit of flapping served as a red cape waved in front of a bull. The boar lowered his tusks and rammed the cow again.

The woman leaned across and beat at the boar's snout.

"Move back!" Reed shouted. "Move back!" He leaped to the ground, yanking his pistol from the holster beneath his arm.

"No! Don't hurt the cow!"

The boar rammed the cow again.

Since the woman still leaned over the downed bovine, the force of the boar's impact catapulted her backward. She hit the rock wall behind her, sliding down to land hard on her butt.

When the boar backed away, preparing for another charge, Reed aimed at the hog's head and fired.

The hog dropped where it stood.

Reed raced to where the woman sat, rubbing the back of her head, her eyes glazed.

"You all right?" He held out a hand.

She ignored him and scrambled to her feet. "Move!" Shoving him to the side, she ran a few steps along the base of the bluff before doubling over and throwing up in the dirt.

Reed hurried over to her and held her hair out of her face until she was done, hesitantly patting her back. He wasn't sure what to do. Something inside him made him want to comfort this woman who'd gone through a particularly scary event.

When she straightened, her face was pale, but her lips were firm. She looked like a woman with a tentative grasp on her control and the determination to maintain it. "Can you give me a hand with the calf? It's stillborn and stuck."

Reed stared into her eyes until he was sure she was going to remain on her feet, then he turned to the laboring cow.

He'd seen this happen before when a cow tried to give birth to a calf too big. Half the time, they lost cow and calf. With the calf already dead, the best they could hope for was to save the cow.

He sat in the dirt behind the cow, braced his feet and grabbed hold of the dead calf's legs.

Too tired and battered to help, the cow lay on her side, breathing hard. When the next contraction hit, she bellowed, and Reed pulled with all his might. The calf slid out a little farther.

"You're doing good." The woman squatted beside the cow and smoothed a hand over her head. "Hang in there."

Another contraction rolled over the cow's belly and her legs stretched straight out, her stomach muscles convulsing.

Reaching down to the calf's shoulders, Reed tugged as hard as he could and the calf slid out the rest of the way.

For several long moments, the cow and Reed gathered their strength. Then the cow rolled to a sitting position and nudged the dead calf.

"Sorry, girl, this baby didn't make it." The woman patted the cow's neck.

Reed stood and wiped his hands on his jeans.

The woman straightened, the top of her head only coming up to Reed's shoulders. "You here about the job?"

"Yes, ma'am."

She eyed the dead boar. "Was I mistaken or did you drop that with one shot?"

"You were not mistaken, ma'am."

She dusted her hands on her jeans and reached out. "I'm Mona Grainger. You're hired."

Chapter Two

The man with the sandy-blond hair, moss-green eyes and a square jawline stood with his cowboy hat in hand, staring at her. "You're M. Grainger? The owner of the Rancho Linda?"

She had to give this guy a little credit. He asked without the usual shocked look. "That would be me." She'd gotten the shocked response from all the applicants thus far. They expected a wiry, grizzled hulk of a man like her father. Not a petite young woman who barely topped five feet three inches.

Her father had died less than a year ago in a riding accident, leaving her as the sole surviving heir to the ranch. She couldn't change her sex or size. What you saw was what you got. "Do you have a problem answering to a female boss?"

"Not at all." He grinned. "I just didn't expect M. Grainger to be so...pretty." He stuck out his hand. "Reed Bryson." He glanced at his dirty hand. "Never mind."

When he started to drop his hand, she grabbed it and shook it with as firm a grip as she could muster. She may be small, but she didn't want him to think she wasn't tough. "A little dirt never hurt me."

Now that she had time to really study him, she wasn't as pleased as she'd been at first to hire him. Although not exactly what she'd hoped for, Mr. Bryson had proven he could ride and shoot, and he hadn't balked at helping a cow with a stillborn calf. The roping part could be taught. It was the rest of the package that bothered her.

Mona's gaze ran the long length of the cowboy who stood at least six feet two in his faded denim jeans and blue chambray shirt. A twinge of apprehension gnawed at her now-empty gut. She didn't like men who were too good to look at. She'd fallen into that trap before and she sure as hell wasn't going there again. Some mistakes were harder to live with than others.

Reed dropped her hand and squatted next to the boar. "Should be good eating. Want me to fieldstrip him?"

The stench of the hog wrapped around her olfactory nerves and her stomach rebelled. For the second time in the past ten minutes, she ran a couple steps and then hurled the last of the contents of her belly.

"On second thought, why don't we get you back to the house. I can come back here later and take care of him and check on the cow."

Fernando raced around the corner, brought his horse to a skidding halt and dropped to the ground. "Miss Mona, are you all right?" He hurried across the floor of the canyon and wrapped an arm around the woman as if she would break.

With a grimace, she pushed him away. "I'm all right. Nothing's broken."

He snatched her hat from the ground and pounded it against his leg before he handed it to her. A deep frown marred his dark forehead. "You should have waited for me to come help you with the cow. It's not something a—"

"I'm fine." She shot a glance at Reed. Fernando worried too much about her and her condition. Let the new hand get adjusted to working for a woman before he learned more about her.

Her foreman followed her glance and nodded. "This kind of work takes more than one to accomplish. Especially when you're in the canyons. Wild boars aren't the only animals you have to worry about."

She knew all too well the risks. But she refused to lose any more livestock to man or beast. Mona turned to the new hand. "When can you start?"

"It seems I've already started." He glanced down at his dirty jeans. "Is today all right with you?"

"Perfect. How are you for working nights?"

"I spent twelve years on the force in Chicago and the past few months as a deputy for Briscoe County. I know how to pull night duty, but tell me—" Reed frowned "—what kind of cattle ranching are you doing at night?"

Her rosy lips twisted. "Call it ranch security." She turned to Fernando. "I don't suppose Sassy stopped at the edge of the canyon, did she?"

"No. She's probably back at the barn by now." He removed his toe from the left stirrup. "You take the saddle. I'll ride behind."

With her bottom bruised from the fall, Mona didn't

argue. She stretched high to reach the saddle horn. Before she knew it, hands grasped her waist and lifted her into the saddle. Hands bigger and stronger than Fernando's.

Heat filled her cheeks as she fitted her boots into the stirrups. She hadn't had someone lift her so effortlessly into a saddle since she was a little girl. And damned if she didn't like it a little too much. A frown settled between her brows. "I can manage on my own."

"Yes, ma'am. I reckon you can, but my mamma taught me to help a lady. It's kind of a habit." As he stared up at her, a smile tipped the corners of his lips.

Her insides warmed, the heat spreading up her neck. Then a gray haze filtered her vision, blackness creeping around the edges. Oh no. Not again.

The blackness claimed her.

* * * * *

Lone star cowboys and secret babies...only Texas is big enough to contain 'em both!
Look for TEXAS-SIZED SECRETS by Elle James, available for a limited time in March 2008 from Harlequin Intrigue.

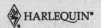

INTRIGUE

SIX NEW PASSIONATE AND THRILLING NOVELS ARE AVAILABLE EACH MONTH.

On sale March 2008

Available wherever books are sold, including most bookstores, supermarkets, drugstores and discount stores.

Receive $1.^{00}$ off

TEXAS-SIZED SECRETS

or any other Harlequin Intrigue novel.

Coupon expires August 1, 2008.
Redeemable at participating retail outlets in the U.S. only.
Limit one coupon per customer.

5 65373 00076 2 (8100) 0 11481

HI08COUP4R

Discover the
Harlequin® Romance novel
that's just right for you.

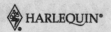

So you've just had a sneak peek...

Tell us what you think and we'll reward you with great savings!

(See details online.)

Visit
www.tellharlequin.com

for your chance to win a free book subscription for a year!